Novella

French literature

ISBN-13 : 978-15-46539-34-6

© Éditions Lambda 2017

GUY DE MAUPASSANT

BOULE DE SUIF

*f*or several days in succession fragments of a defeated army had passed through the town. They were mere disorganized bands, not disciplined forces. The men wore long, dirty beards and tattered uniforms; they advanced in listless fashion, without a flag, without a leader. All seemed exhausted, worn out, incapable of thought or resolve, marching onward merely by force of habit, and dropping to the ground with fatigue the moment they halted. One saw, in particular, many enlisted men, peaceful citizens, men who lived quietly on their income, bending beneath the weight of their rifles; and little active volunteers, easily frightened but full of enthusiasm, as eager to attack as they were ready to take to flight; and amid these, a sprinkling of red-breeched soldiers, the pitiful remnant of a division cut down in a great battle; somber artillerymen, side by side with nondescript foot-soldiers; and, here and there, the gleaming helmet of a heavy-footed dragoon who had difficulty in keeping up with the quicker pace of the soldiers of the line. Legions of irregulars with high-sounding names "Avengers of Defeat," "Citizens of the Tomb," "Brethren in Death"—passed in their turn, looking like banditti. Their leaders, former drapers or grain merchants, or tallow or soap chandlers—warriors by force of circumstances, officers by reason of their mustachios or their money—covered with weapons, flannel and gold lace, spoke in an impressive manner, discussed plans of campaign, and behaved as though they alone bore the fortunes of dying France on their braggart shoulders; though, in truth, they frequently were afraid of their own men—scoundrels often brave beyond measure, but pillagers and debauchees.

Rumor had it that the Prussians were about to enter Rouen.

The members of the National Guard, who for the past two months had been reconnoitering with the utmost caution in the neighboring woods, occasionally shooting their own sentinels, and making ready for fight whenever a rabbit rustled in the undergrowth, had now returned to their homes. Their arms, their uniforms, all the death-dealing paraphernalia with which they had terrified all the milestones along the highroad for eight miles round, had suddenly and marvellously disappeared.

The last of the French soldiers had just crossed the Seine on their way to Pont-Audemer, through

Saint-Sever and Bourg-Achard, and in their rear the vanquished general, powerless to do aught with the forlorn remnants of his army, himself dismayed at the final overthrow of a nation accustomed to victory and disastrously beaten despite its legendary bravery, walked between two orderlies.

Then a profound calm, a shuddering, silent dread, settled on the city. Many a round-paunched citizen, emasculated by years devoted to business, anxiously awaited the conquerors, trembling lest his roasting-jacks or kitchen knives should be looked upon as weapons.

Life seemed to have stopped short; the shops were shut, the streets deserted. Now and then an inhabitant, awed by the silence, glided swiftly by in the shadow of the walls. The anguish of suspense made men even desire the arrival of the enemy.

In the afternoon of the day following the departure of the French troops, a number of uhlans, coming no one knew whence, passed rapidly through the town. A little later on, a black mass descended St. Catherine's Hill, while two other invading bodies appeared respectively on the Darnetal and the Boisguillaume roads. The advance guards of the three corps arrived at precisely the same moment at the Square of the Hotel de Ville, and the German army poured through all the adjacent streets, its battalions making the pavement ring with their firm, measured tread.

Orders shouted in an unknown, guttural tongue rose to the windows of the seemingly dead, deserted houses; while behind the fast-closed shutters eager eyes peered forth at the victors-masters now of the city, its fortunes, and its lives, by "right of war." The inhabitants, in their darkened rooms, were possessed by that terror which follows in the wake of cataclysms, of deadly upheavals of the earth, against which all human skill and strength are vain. For the same thing happens whenever the established order of things is upset, when security no longer exists, when all those rights usually protected by the law of man or of Nature are at the mercy of unreasoning, savage force. The earthquake crushing a whole nation under falling roofs; the flood let loose, and engulfing in its swirling depths the corpses of drowned peasants, along with dead oxen and beams torn from shattered houses; or the army, covered with glory, murdering those who defend themselves, making prisoners of the rest, pillaging in the name of the Sword, and giving thanks to God to the thunder of cannon — all these are appalling scourges, which destroy all belief in eternal justice, all that confidence we have been taught to feel in the protection of Heaven and the reason of man.

Small detachments of soldiers knocked at each door, and then disappeared within the houses; for the vanquished saw they would have to be civil to their conquerors.

At the end of a short time, once the first terror had subsided, calm was again restored. In many houses the Prussian officer ate at the same table with the family. He was often well-bred, and, out of politeness, expressed sympathy with France and repugnance at being compelled to take part in the war. This sentiment was received with gratitude; besides, his protection might be needful some day or other. By the exercise of tact the number of men quartered in one's house might be reduced; and why should one provoke the hostility of a person on whom one's whole welfare depended? Such conduct would savor less of bravery than of foolhardiness. And foolhardiness is no longer a failing of the citizens of Rouen as it was in the days when their city earned renown by its heroic defenses. Last of all—final argument based on the national politeness—the folk of Rouen said to one another that it was only right to be civil in one's own house, provided there was no public exhibition of familiarity with the foreigner. Out of doors, therefore, citizen and soldier did not know each other; but in the house both chatted freely, and each evening the German remained a little longer warming himself at the hospitable hearth.

Even the town itself resumed by degrees its ordinary aspect. The French seldom walked abroad, but the streets swarmed with Prussian soldiers. Moreover, the officers of the Blue Hussars, who arrogantly dragged

their instruments of death along the pavements, seemed
to hold the simple townsmen in but little more contempt
than did the French cavalry officers who had drunk at
the same cafes the year before.

But there was something in the air, a something strange
and subtle, an intolerable foreign atmosphere like a
penetrating odor—the odor of invasion. It permeated
dwellings and places of public resort, changed the taste
of food, made one imagine one's self in far-distant lands,
amid dangerous, barbaric tribes.

The conquerors exacted money, much money. The
inhabitants paid what was asked; they were rich. But,
the wealthier a Norman tradesman becomes, the more
he suffers at having to part with anything that belongs
to him, at having to see any portion of his substance
pass into the hands of another.

Nevertheless, within six or seven miles of the town,
along the course of the river as it flows onward to
Croisset, Dieppedalle and Biessart, boat-men and
fishermen often hauled to the surface of the water the
body of a German, bloated in his uniform, killed by a
blow from knife or club, his head crushed by a stone,
or perchance pushed from some bridge into the stream
below. The mud of the river-bed swallowed up these
obscure acts of vengeance—savage, yet legitimate;
these unrecorded deeds of bravery; these silent attacks
fraught with greater danger than battles fought in

broad day, and surrounded, moreover, with no halo of romance. For hatred of the foreigner ever arms a few intrepid souls, ready to die for an idea.

At last, as the invaders, though subjecting the town to the strictest discipline, had not committed any of the deeds of horror with which they had been credited while on their triumphal march, the people grew bolder, and the necessities of business again animated the breasts of the local merchants. Some of these had important commercial interests at Havre —occupied at present by the French army—and wished to attempt to reach that port by overland route to Dieppe, taking the boat from there.

Through the influence of the German officers whose acquaintance they had made, they obtained a permit to leave town from the general in command.

A large four-horse coach having, therefore, been engaged for the journey, and ten passengers having given in their names to the proprietor, they decided to start on a certain Tuesday morning before daybreak, to avoid attracting a crowd.

The ground had been frozen hard for some time-past, and about three o'clock on Monday afternoon—large black clouds from the north shed their burden of snow uninterruptedly all through that evening and night.

At half-past four in the morning the travellers met in

the courtyard of the Hotel de Normandie, where they were to take their seats in the coach.

They were still half asleep, and shivering with cold under their wraps. They could see one another but indistinctly in the darkness, and the mountain of heavy winter wraps in which each was swathed made them look like a gathering of obese priests in their long cassocks. But two men recognized each other, a third accosted them, and the three began to talk. "I am bringing my wife," said one. "So am I." "And I, too." The first speaker added: "We shall not return to Rouen, and if the Prussians approach Havre we will cross to England." All three, it turned out, had made the same plans, being of similar disposition and temperament.

Still the horses were not harnessed. A small lantern carried by a stable-boy emerged now and then from one dark doorway to disappear immediately in another. The stamping of horses' hoofs, deadened by the dung and straw of the stable, was heard from time to time, and from inside the building issued a man's voice, talking to the animals and swearing at them. A faint tinkle of bells showed that the harness was being got ready; this tinkle soon developed into a continuous jingling, louder or softer according to the movements of the horse, sometimes stopping altogether, then breaking out in a sudden peal accompanied by a pawing of the ground by an iron-shod hoof.

The door suddenly closed. All noise ceased.

The frozen townsmen were silent; they remained motionless, stiff with cold.

A thick curtain of glistening white flakes fell ceaselessly to the ground; it obliterated all outlines, enveloped all objects in an icy mantle of foam; nothing was to be heard throughout the length and breadth of the silent, winter-bound city save the vague, nameless rustle of falling snow — a sensation rather than a sound — the gentle mingling of light atoms which seemed to fill all space, to cover the whole world.

The man reappeared with his lantern, leading by a rope a melancholy-looking horse, evidently being led out against his inclination. The hostler placed him beside the pole, fastened the traces, and spent some time in walking round him to make sure that the harness was all right; for he could use only one hand, the other being engaged in holding the lantern. As he was about to fetch the second horse he noticed the motionless group of travellers, already white with snow, and said to them: "Why don't you get inside the coach? You'd be under shelter, at least."

This did not seem to have occurred to them, and they at once took his advice. The three men seated their wives at the far end of the coach, then got in themselves; lastly the other vague, snow-shrouded forms clambered to the remaining places without a word.

The floor was covered with straw, into which the feet sank. The ladies at the far end, having brought with them little copper foot-warmers heated by means of a kind of chemical fuel, proceeded to light these, and spent some time in expatiating in low tones on their advantages, saying over and over again things which they had all known for a long time.

At last, six horses instead of four having been harnessed to the diligence, on account of the heavy roads, a voice outside asked: "Is every one there?" To which a voice from the interior replied: "Yes," and they set out.

The vehicle moved slowly, slowly, at a snail's pace; the wheels sank into the snow; the entire body of the coach creaked and groaned; the horses slipped, puffed, steamed, and the coachman's long whip cracked incessantly, flying hither and thither, coiling up, then flinging out its length like a slender serpent, as it lashed some rounded flank, which instantly grew tense as it strained in further effort.

But the day grew apace. Those light flakes which one traveller, a native of Rouen, had compared to a rain of cotton fell no longer. A murky light filtered through dark, heavy clouds, which made the country more dazzlingly white by contrast, a whiteness broken sometimes by a row of tall trees spangled with hoarfrost, or by a cottage roof hooded in snow.

Within the coach the passengers eyed one another curiously in the dim light of dawn.

Right at the back, in the best seats of all, Monsieur and Madame Loiseau, wholesale wine merchants of the Rue Grand-Pont, slumbered opposite each other. Formerly clerk to a merchant who had failed in business, Loiseau had bought his master's interest, and made a fortune for himself. He sold very bad wine at a very low price to the retail-dealers in the country, and had the reputation, among his friends and acquaintances, of being a shrewd rascal a true Norman, full of quips and wiles. So well established was his character as a cheat that, in the mouths of the citizens of Rouen, the very name of Loiseau became a byword for sharp practice.

Above and beyond this, Loiseau was noted for his practical jokes of every description—his tricks, good or ill-natured; and no one could mention his name without adding at once: "He's an extraordinary man—Loiseau." He was undersized and potbellied, had a florid face with grayish whiskers.

His wife-tall, strong, determined, with a loud voice and decided manner —represented the spirit of order and arithmetic in the business house which Loiseau enlivened by his jovial activity.

Beside them, dignified in bearing, belonging to a superior caste, sat Monsieur Carre-Lamadon, a man of considerable importance, a king in the cotton trade, proprietor of three spinning-mills, officer of the Legion of Honor, and member of the General Council. During the whole time the Empire was in the ascendancy he remained the chief of the well-disposed Opposition, merely in order to command a higher value for his devotion when he should rally to the cause which he meanwhile opposed with "courteous weapons," to use his own expression.

Madame Carre-Lamadon, much younger than her husband, was the consolation of all the officers of good family quartered at Rouen. Pretty, slender, graceful, she sat opposite her husband, curled up in her furs, and gazing mournfully at the sorry interior of the coach.

Her neighbors, the Comte and Comtesse Hubert de Breville, bore one of the noblest and most ancient names in Normandy. The count, a nobleman advanced in years and of aristocratic bearing, strove to enhance by every artifice of the toilet, his natural resemblance to King Henry IV, who, according to a legend of which the family were inordinately proud, had been the favored lover of a De Breville lady, and father of her child —the frail one's husband having, in recognition of this fact, been made a count and governor of a province.

A colleague of Monsieur Carre-Lamadon in the General Council, Count Hubert represented the Orleanist party in his department. The story of his marriage with the daughter of a small shipowner at Nantes had always remained more or less of a mystery. But as the countess had an air of unmistakable breeding, entertained faultlessly, and was even supposed to have been loved by a son of Louis-Philippe, the nobility vied with one another in doing her honor, and her drawing-room remained the most select in the whole countryside—the only one which retained the old spirit of gallantry, and to which access was not easy.

The fortune of the Brevilles, all in real estate, amounted, it was said, to five hundred thousand francs a year.

These six people occupied the farther end of the coach, and represented Society—with an income—the strong, established society of good people with religion and principle.

It happened by chance that all the women were seated on the same side; and the countess had, moreover, as neighbors two nuns, who spent the time in fingering their long rosaries and murmuring paternosters and aves. One of them was old, and so deeply pitted with smallpox that she looked for all the world as if she had received a charge of shot full in the face. The other, of sickly appearance, had a pretty but wasted countenance, and a narrow, consumptive chest, sapped by that devouring faith which is the making of martyrs and visionaries.

A man and woman, sitting opposite the two nuns, attracted all eyes.

The man—a well-known character—was Cornudet, the democrat, the terror of all respectable people. For the past twenty years his big red beard had been on terms of intimate acquaintance with the tankards of all the republican cafes. With the help of his comrades and brethren he had dissipated a respectable fortune left him by his father, an old-established confectioner, and he now impatiently awaited the Republic, that he might at last be rewarded with the post he had earned by his revolutionary orgies. On the fourth of September— possibly as the result of a practical joke—he was led to believe that he had been appointed prefect; but when he attempted to take up the duties of the position the clerks in charge of the office refused to recognize his authority, and he was compelled in consequence to retire. A good sort of fellow in other respects, inoffensive and obliging, he had thrown himself zealously into the work of making an organized defence of the town. He had had pits dug in the level country, young forest trees felled, and traps set on all the roads; then at the approach of the enemy, thoroughly satisfied with his preparations, he had hastily returned to the town. He thought he might now do more good at Havre, where new intrenchments would soon be necessary.

The woman, who belonged to the courtesan class,

was celebrated for an embonpoint unusual for her age, which had earned for her the sobriquet of "Boule de Suif"[1]. Short and round, fat as a pig, with puffy fingers constricted at the joints, looking like rows of short sausages; with a shiny, tightly-stretched skin and an enormous bust filling out the bodice of her dress, she was yet attractive and much sought after, owing to her fresh and pleasing appearance. Her face was like a crimson apple, a peony-bud just bursting into bloom; she had two magnificent dark eyes, fringed with thick, heavy lashes, which cast a shadow into their depths; her mouth was small, ripe, kissable, and was furnished with the tiniest of white teeth.

As soon as she was recognized the respectable matrons of the party began to whisper among themselves, and the words "hussy" and "public scandal" were uttered so loudly that Boule de Suif raised her head. She forthwith cast such a challenging, bold look at her neighbors that a sudden silence fell on the company, and all lowered their eyes, with the exception of Loiseau, who watched her with evident interest.

But conversation was soon resumed among the three ladies, whom the presence of this girl had suddenly drawn together in the bonds of friendship—one might almost say in those of intimacy. They decided that they ought to combine, as it were, in their dignity as wives in

---

1. *Tallow Ball.*

face of this shameless hussy; for legitimized love always despises its easygoing brother.

The three men, also, brought together by a certain conservative instinct awakened by the presence of Cornudet, spoke of money matters in a tone expressive of contempt for the poor. Count Hubert related the losses he had sustained at the hands of the Prussians, spoke of the cattle which had been stolen from him, the crops which had been ruined, with the easy manner of a nobleman who was also a tenfold millionaire, and whom such reverses would scarcely inconvenience for a single year. Monsieur Carre-Lamadon, a man of wide experience in the cotton industry, had taken care to send six hundred thousand francs to England as provision against the rainy day he was always anticipating. As for Loiseau, he had managed to sell to the French commissariat department all the wines he had in stock, so that the state now owed him a considerable sum, which he hoped to receive at Havre.

And all three eyed one another in friendly, well-disposed fashion. Although of varying social status, they were united in the brotherhood of money—in that vast freemasonry made up of those who possess, who can jingle gold wherever they choose to put their hands into their breeches' pockets.

The coach went along so slowly that at ten o'clock in the morning it had not covered twelve miles. Three times the men of the party got out and climbed the hills on foot. The passengers were becoming uneasy, for they had counted on lunching at Totes, and it seemed now as if they would hardly arrive there before nightfall. Every one was eagerly looking out for an inn by the roadside, when, suddenly, the coach foundered in a snowdrift, and it took two hours to extricate it.

As appetites increased, their spirits fell; no inn, no wine shop could be discovered, the approach of the Prussians and the transit of the starving French troops having frightened away all business.

The men sought food in the farmhouses beside the road, but could not find so much as a crust of bread; for the suspicious peasant invariably hid his stores for fear of being pillaged by the soldiers, who, being entirely without food, would take violent possession of everything they found.

About one o'clock Loiseau announced that he positively had a big hollow in his stomach. They had all been suffering in the same way for some time, and the increasing gnawings of hunger had put an end to all conversation.

Now and then some one yawned, another followed his example, and each in turn, according to his character, breeding and social position, yawned either quietly or noisily, placing his hand before the gaping void whence issued breath condensed into vapor.

Several times Boule de Suif stooped, as if searching for something under her petticoats. She would hesitate a moment, look at her neighbors, and then quietly sit upright again. All faces were pale and drawn. Loiseau declared he would give a thousand francs for a knuckle of ham. His wife made an involuntary and quickly checked gesture of protest. It always hurt her to hear of money being squandered, and she could not even understand jokes on such a subject.

"As a matter of fact, I don't feel well," said the count. "Why did I not think of bringing provisions?" Each one reproached himself in similar fashion.

Cornudet, however, had a bottle of rum, which he offered to his neighbors. They all coldly refused except Loiseau, who took a sip, and returned the bottle with thanks, saying: "That's good stuff; it warms one up, and cheats the appetite." The alcohol put him in good humor, and he proposed they should do as the sailors did in the song: eat the fattest of the passengers. This indirect allusion to Boule de Suif shocked the respectable members of the party. No one replied; only Cornudet smiled. The two good sisters had ceased to mumble their rosary, and, with hands enfolded in their wide sleeves, sat motionless, their eyes steadfastly cast down, doubtless offering up as a sacrifice to Heaven the suffering it had sent them.

At last, at three o'clock, as they were in the midst of an apparently limitless plain, with not a single village in sight, Boule de Suif stooped quickly, and drew from underneath the seat a large basket covered with a white napkin.

From this she extracted first of all a small earthenware plate and a silver drinking cup, then an enormous dish containing two whole chickens cut into joints and imbedded in jelly. The basket was seen to contain other good things: pies, fruit, dainties of all sorts-provisions, in fine, for a three days' journey, rendering their owner independent of wayside inns. The necks of four bottles protruded from among the food. She took a chicken wing, and began to eat it daintily, together with one of those rolls called in Normandy "Regence."

All looks were directed toward her. An odor of food filled the air, causing nostrils to dilate, mouths to water, and jaws to contract painfully. The scorn of the ladies for this disreputable female grew positively ferocious; they would have liked to kill her, or throw, her and her drinking cup, her basket, and her provisions, out of the coach into the snow of the road below.

But Loiseau's gaze was fixed greedily on the dish of chicken. He said:

"Well, well, this lady had more forethought than the rest of us. Some people think of everything."

She looked up at him.

"Would you like some, sir? It is hard to go on fasting all day."

He bowed.

"Upon my soul, I can't refuse; I cannot hold out another minute. All is fair in war time, is it not, madame?" And, casting a glance on those around, he added:

"At times like this it is very pleasant to meet with obliging people."

He spread a newspaper over his knees to avoid soiling his trousers, and, with a pocketknife he always carried, helped himself to a chicken leg coated with jelly, which he thereupon proceeded to devour.

Then Boule le Suif, in low, humble tones, invited the nuns to partake of her repast. They both accepted the offer unhesitatingly, and after a few stammered words of thanks began to eat quickly, without raising their eyes. Neither did Cornudet refuse his neighbor's offer, and, in combination with the nuns, a sort of table was formed by opening out the newspaper over the four pairs of knees.

Mouths kept opening and shutting, ferociously masticating and devouring the food. Loiseau, in his corner, was hard at work, and in low tones urged his wife to follow his example. She held out for a long time, but overstrained Nature gave way at last. Her husband, assuming his politest manner, asked their "charming companion" if he might be allowed to offer Madame Loiseau a small helping.

"Why, certainly, sir," she replied, with an amiable smile, holding out the dish.

When the first bottle of claret was opened some embarrassment was caused by the fact that there was only one drinking cup, but this was passed from one to another, after being wiped. Cornudet alone, doubtless in a spirit of gallantry, raised to his own lips that part of the rim which was still moist from those of his fair neighbor.

Then, surrounded by people who were eating, and well-nigh suffocated by the odor of food, the Comte and Comtesse de Breville and Monsieur and Madame Carre-Lamadon endured that hateful form of torture which has perpetuated the name of Tantalus. All at once the manufacturer's young wife heaved a sigh which made every one turn and look at her; she was white as the snow without; her eyes closed, her head fell forward; she had fainted. Her husband, beside himself, implored the help of his neighbors. No one seemed to know what to do until the elder of the two nuns, raising the patient's head, placed Boule de Suif's drinking cup to her lips, and made her swallow a few drops of wine. The pretty invalid moved, opened her eyes, smiled, and declared in a feeble voice that she was all right again.

But, to prevent a recurrence of the catastrophe, the nun made her drink a cupful of claret, adding: "It's just hunger — that's what is wrong with you."

Then Boule de Suif, blushing and embarrassed, stammered, looking at the four passengers who were still fasting:

"'Mon Dieu', if I might offer these ladies and gentlemen — —"

She stopped short, fearing a snub. But Loiseau continued:

"Hang it all, in such a case as this we are all brothers and sisters and ought to assist each other. Come, come, ladies, don't stand on ceremony, for goodness' sake! Do we even know whether we shall find a house in which to pass the night? At our present rate of going we sha'n't be at Totes till midday to-morrow."

They hesitated, no one daring to be the first to accept. But the count settled the question. He turned toward the abashed girl, and in his most distinguished manner said:

"We accept gratefully, madame."

As usual, it was only the first step that cost. This Rubicon once crossed, they set to work with a will. The basket was emptied. It still contained a pate de foie gras, a lark pie, a piece of smoked tongue, Crassane pears, Pont-Leveque gingerbread, fancy cakes, and a cup full of pickled gherkins and onions — Boule de Suif, like all women, being very fond of indigestible things.

They could not eat this girl's provisions without speaking to her. So they began to talk, stiffly at first; then, as she seemed by no means forward, with greater freedom. Mesdames de Breville and Carre-Lamadon, who were accomplished women of the world, were gracious and tactful. The countess especially displayed that amiable condescension characteristic of great ladies whom no contact with baser mortals can sully, and was absolutely charming. But the sturdy Madame Loiseau, who had the soul of a gendarme, continued morose, speaking little and eating much.

Conversation naturally turned on the war. Terrible stories were told about the Prussians, deeds of bravery were recounted of the French; and all these people who were fleeing themselves were ready to pay homage to the courage of their compatriots. Personal experiences soon followed, and Bottle le Suif related with genuine emotion, and with that warmth of language not uncommon in women of her class and temperament, how it came about that she had left Rouen.

"I thought at first that I should be able to stay," she said. "My house was well stocked with provisions, and it seemed better to put up with feeding a few soldiers than to banish myself goodness knows where. But when I saw these Prussians it was too much for me! My blood

boiled with rage; I wept the whole day for very shame.
Oh, if only I had been a man! I looked at them from my
window—the fat swine, with their pointed helmets!—
and my maid held my hands to keep me from throwing
my furniture down on them. Then some of them were
quartered on me; I flew at the throat of the first one
who entered. They are just as easy to strangle as other
men! And I'd have been the death of that one if I hadn't
been dragged away from him by my hair. I had to hide
after that. And as soon as I could get an opportunity I
left the place, and here I am."

She was warmly congratulated. She rose in the
estimation of her companions, who had not been so
brave; and Cornudet listened to her with the approving
and benevolent smile of an apostle, the smile a priest
might wear in listening to a devotee praising God; for
long-bearded democrats of his type have a monopoly of
patriotism, just as priests have a monopoly of religion.
He held forth in turn, with dogmatic self-assurance,
in the style of the proclamations daily pasted on the
walls of the town, winding up with a specimen of stump
oratory in which he reviled "that besotted fool of a
Louis-Napoleon."

But Boule de Suif was indignant, for she was an
ardent Bonapartist. She turned as red as a cherry, and
stammered in her wrath: "I'd just like to have seen you
in his place—you and your sort! There would have

been a nice mix-up. Oh, yes! It was you who betrayed that man. It would be impossible to live in France if we were governed by such rascals as you!"

Cornudet, unmoved by this tirade, still smiled a superior, contemptuous smile; and one felt that high words were impending, when the count interposed, and, not without difficulty, succeeded in calming the exasperated woman, saying that all sincere opinions ought to be respected. But the countess and the manufacturer's wife, imbued with the unreasoning hatred of the upper classes for the Republic, and instinct, moreover, with the affection felt by all women for the pomp and circumstance of despotic government, were drawn, in spite of themselves, toward this dignified young woman, whose opinions coincided so closely with their own.

The basket was empty. The ten people had finished its contents without difficulty amid general regret that it did not hold more. Conversation went on a little longer, though it flagged somewhat after the passengers had finished eating.

Night fell, the darkness grew deeper and deeper, and the cold made Boule de Suif shiver, in spite of her plumpness. So Madame de Breville offered her her foot-warmer, the fuel of which had been several times renewed since the morning, and she accepted the offer at once, for her feet were icy cold. Mesdames Carre-Lamadon and Loiseau gave theirs to the nuns.

The driver lighted his lanterns. They cast a bright gleam on a cloud of vapor which hovered over the sweating flanks of the horses, and on the roadside snow, which seemed to unroll as they went along in the changing light of the lamps.

All was now indistinguishable in the coach; but suddenly a movement occurred in the corner occupied by Boule de Suif and Cornudet; and Loiseau, peering into the gloom, fancied he saw the big, bearded democrat move hastily to one side, as if he had received a well-directed, though noiseless, blow in the dark.

Tiny lights glimmered ahead. It was Totes. The coach had been on the road eleven hours, which, with the three hours allotted the horses in four periods for feeding and breathing, made fourteen. It entered the town, and stopped before the Hotel du Commerce.

The coach door opened; a well-known noise made all the travellers start; it was the clanging of a scabbard, on the pavement; then a voice called out something in German.

Although the coach had come to a standstill, no one got out; it looked as if they were afraid of being murdered the moment they left their seats. Thereupon the driver appeared, holding in his hand one of his lanterns, which cast a sudden glow on the interior of the coach, lighting up the double row of startled faces, mouths agape, and eyes wide open in surprise and terror.

Beside the driver stood in the full light a German officer, a tall young man, fair and slender, tightly encased in his uniform like a woman in her corset, his flat shiny cap, tilted to one side of his head, making him look like an English hotel runner. His exaggerated mustache, long and straight and tapering to a point at either end in a single blond hair that could hardly be seen, seemed to weigh down the corners of his mouth and give a droop to his lips.

In Alsatian French he requested the travellers to alight, saying stiffly:

"Kindly get down, ladies and gentlemen."

The two nuns were the first to obey, manifesting the docility of holy women accustomed to submission on every occasion. Next appeared the count and countess, followed by the manufacturer and his wife, after whom came Loiseau, pushing his larger and better half before him.

"Good-day, sir," he said to the officer as he put his foot to the ground, acting on an impulse born of prudence rather than of politeness. The other, insolent like all in authority, merely stared without replying.

Boule de Suif and Cornudet, though near the door,

were the last to alight, grave and dignified before the enemy. The stout girl tried to control herself and appear calm; the democrat stroked his long russet beard with a somewhat trembling hand. Both strove to maintain their dignity, knowing well that at such a time each individual is always looked upon as more or less typical of his nation; and, also, resenting the complaisant attitude of their companions, Boule de Suif tried to wear a bolder front than her neighbors, the virtuous women, while he, feeling that it was incumbent on him to set a good example, kept up the attitude of resistance which he had first assumed when he undertook to mine the high roads round Rouen.

They entered the spacious kitchen of the inn, and the German, having demanded the passports signed by the general in command, in which were mentioned the name, description and profession of each traveller, inspected them all minutely, comparing their appearance with the written particulars.

Then he said brusquely: "All right," and turned on his heel.

They breathed freely, All were still hungry; so supper was ordered. Half an hour was required for its preparation, and while two servants were apparently engaged in getting it ready the travellers went to look at their rooms. These all opened off a long corridor, at the end of which was a glazed door with a number on it.

They were just about to take their seats at table when the innkeeper appeared in person. He was a former horse dealer—a large, asthmatic individual, always wheezing, coughing, and clearing his throat. Follenvie was his patronymic.

He called:

"Mademoiselle Elisabeth Rousset?"

Boule de Suif started, and turned round.

"That is my name."

"Mademoiselle, the Prussian officer wishes to speak to you immediately."

"To me?"

"Yes; if you are Mademoiselle Elisabeth Rousset."

She hesitated, reflected a moment, and then declared roundly:

"That may be; but I'm not going."

They moved restlessly around her; every one wondered and speculated as to the cause of this order. The count approached:

"You are wrong, madame, for your refusal may bring trouble not only on yourself but also on all your companions. It never pays to resist those in authority. Your compliance with this request cannot possibly be fraught with any danger; it has probably been made because some formality or other was forgotten."

All added their voices to that of the count; Boule de Suif was begged, urged, lectured, and at last convinced; every one was afraid of the complications which might result from headstrong action on her part. She said finally:

"I am doing it for your sakes, remember that!"

The countess took her hand.

"And we are grateful to you."

She left the room. All waited for her return before commencing the meal. Each was distressed that he or she had not been sent for rather than this impulsive, quick-tempered girl, and each mentally rehearsed platitudes in case of being summoned also.

But at the end of ten minutes she reappeared breathing hard, crimson with indignation.

"Oh! the scoundrel! the scoundrel!" she stammered.

All were anxious to know what had happened; but she declined to enlighten them, and when the count pressed the point, she silenced him with much dignity, saying:

"No; the matter has nothing to do with you, and I cannot speak of it."

Then they took their places round a high soup tureen,

from which issued an odor of cabbage. In spite of this coincidence, the supper was cheerful. The cider was good; the Loiseaus and the nuns drank it from motives of economy. The others ordered wine; Cornudet demanded beer. He had his own fashion of uncorking the bottle and making the beer foam, gazing at it as he inclined his glass and then raised it to a position between the lamp and his eye that he might judge of its color. When he drank, his great beard, which matched the color of his favorite beverage, seemed to tremble with affection; his eyes positively squinted in the endeavor not to lose sight of the beloved glass, and he looked for all the world as if he were fulfilling the only function for which he was born. He seemed to have established in his mind an affinity between the two great passions of his life—pale ale and revolution—and assuredly he could not taste the one without dreaming of the other.

Monsieur and Madame Follenvie dined at the end of the table. The man, wheezing like a broken-down locomotive, was too short-winded to talk when he was eating. But the wife was not silent a moment; she told how the Prussians had impressed her on their arrival, what they did, what they said; execrating them in the first place because they cost her money, and in the second because she had two sons in the army. She addressed herself principally to the countess, flattered at the opportunity of talking to a lady of quality.

Then she lowered her voice, and began to broach delicate subjects. Her husband interrupted her from time to time, saying:

"You would do well to hold your tongue, Madame Follenvie."

But she took no notice of him, and went on:

"Yes, madame, these Germans do nothing but eat potatoes and pork, and then pork and potatoes. And don't imagine for a moment that they are clean! No, indeed! And if only you saw them drilling for hours, indeed for days, together; they all collect in a field, then they do nothing but march backward and forward, and wheel this way and that. If only they would cultivate the land, or remain at home and work on their high roads! Really, madame, these soldiers are of no earthly use! Poor people have to feed and keep them, only in order that they may learn how to kill! True, I am only an old woman with no education, but when I see them wearing themselves out marching about from morning till night, I say to myself: When there are people who make discoveries that are of use to people, why should others take so much trouble to do harm? Really, now, isn't it a terrible thing to kill people, whether they are Prussians, or English, or Poles, or French? If we revenge ourselves on any one who injures us we do wrong, and are punished for it; but when our sons are shot down like partridges, that is all right, and decorations are given to the man who kills the most. No, indeed, I shall never be able to understand it."

Cornudet raised his voice:

"War is a barbarous proceeding when we attack a peaceful neighbor, but it is a sacred duty when undertaken in defence of one's country."

The old woman looked down:

"Yes; it's another matter when one acts in self-defence; but would it not be better to kill all the kings, seeing that they make war just to amuse themselves?"

Cornudet's eyes kindled.

"Bravo, citizens!" he said.

Monsieur Carre-Lamadon was reflecting profoundly. Although an ardent admirer of great generals, the peasant woman's sturdy common sense made him reflect on the wealth which might accrue to a country by the employment of so many idle hands now maintained at a great expense, of so much unproductive force, if they were employed in those great industrial enterprises which it will take centuries to complete.

But Loiseau, leaving his seat, went over to the innkeeper and began chatting in a low voice. The big man chuckled, coughed, sputtered; his enormous carcass shook with merriment at the pleasantries of the other; and he ended by buying six casks of claret from

Loiseau to be delivered in spring, after the departure of the Prussians.

The moment supper was over every one went to bed, worn out with fatigue.

But Loiseau, who had been making his observations on the sly, sent his wife to bed, and amused himself by placing first his ear, and then his eye, to the bedroom keyhole, in order to discover what he called "the mysteries of the corridor."

At the end of about an hour he heard a rustling, peeped out quickly, and caught sight of Boule de Suif, looking more rotund than ever in a dressing-gown of blue cashmere trimmed with white lace. She held a candle in her hand, and directed her steps to the numbered door at the end of the corridor. But one of the side doors was partly opened, and when, at the end of a few minutes, she returned, Cornudet, in his shirt-sleeves, followed her. They spoke in low tones, then stopped short. Boule de Suif seemed to be stoutly denying him admission to her room. Unfortunately, Loiseau could not at first hear what they said; but toward the end of the conversation they raised their voices, and he caught a few words. Cornudet was loudly insistent.

"How silly you are! What does it matter to you?" he said.

She seemed indignant, and replied:

"No, my good man, there are times when one does not do that sort of thing; besides, in this place it would be shameful."

Apparently he did not understand, and asked the reason. Then she lost her temper and her caution, and, raising her voice still higher, said:

"Why? Can't you understand why? When there are Prussians in the house! Perhaps even in the very next room!"

He was silent. The patriotic shame of this wanton, who would not suffer herself to be caressed in the neighborhood of the enemy, must have roused his dormant dignity, for after bestowing on her a simple kiss he crept softly back to his room. Loiseau, much edified, capered round the bedroom before taking his place beside his slumbering spouse.

Then silence reigned throughout the house. But soon there arose from some remote part—it might easily have been either cellar or attic—a stertorous, monotonous, regular snoring, a dull, prolonged rumbling, varied by tremors like those of a boiler under pressure of steam. Monsieur Follenvie had gone to sleep.

As they had decided on starting at eight o'clock the next morning, every one was in the kitchen at that hour; but the coach, its roof covered with snow, stood by itself in the middle of the yard, without either horses or driver. They sought the latter in the stables, coach-houses and barns —but in vain. So the men of the party resolved to scour the country for him, and sallied forth. They found them selves in the square, with the church at the farther side, and to right and left low-roofed houses where there were some Prussian soldiers. The first soldier they saw was peeling potatoes. The second, farther on, was washing out a barber's shop. An other, bearded to the eyes, was fondling a crying infant, and dandling it on his knees to quiet it; and the stout peasant women, whose men-folk were for the most part at the war, were, by means of signs, telling their obedient conquerors what work they were to do: chop wood, prepare soup, grind coffee; one of them even was doing the washing for his hostess, an infirm old grandmother.

The count, astonished at what he saw, questioned the beadle who was coming out of the presbytery. The old man answered:

"Oh, those men are not at all a bad sort; they are not Prussians, I am told; they come from somewhere farther off, I don't exactly know where. And they have all left wives and children behind them; they are not fond of war either, you may be sure! I am sure they are mourning for the men where they come from, just as we do here; and the war causes them just as much unhappiness as it does us. As a matter of fact, things are not so very bad here just now, because the soldiers do no harm, and work just as if they were in their own homes. You see, sir, poor folk always help one another; it is the great ones of this world who make war."

Cornudet indignant at the friendly understanding established between conquerors and conquered, withdrew, preferring to shut himself up in the inn.

"They are repeopling the country," jested Loiseau.

"They are undoing the harm they have done," said Monsieur Carre-Lamadon gravely.

But they could not find the coach driver. At last he was discovered in the village cafe, fraternizing cordially with the officer's orderly.

"Were you not told to harness the horses at eight o'clock?" demanded the count.

"Oh, yes; but I've had different orders since."

"What orders?"

"Not to harness at all."

"Who gave you such orders?"

"Why, the Prussian officer."

"But why?"

"I don't know. Go and ask him. I am forbidden to harness the horses, so I don't harness them — that's all."

"Did he tell you so himself?"

"No, sir; the innkeeper gave me the order from him."

"When?"

"Last evening, just as I was going to bed."

The three men returned in a very uneasy frame of mind.

They asked for Monsieur Follenvie, but the servant replied that on account of his asthma he never got up before ten o'clock. They were strictly forbidden to rouse him earlier, except in case of fire.

They wished to see the officer, but that also was impossible, although he lodged in the inn. Monsieur Follenvie alone was authorized to interview him on civil matters. So they waited. The women returned to their rooms, and occupied themselves with trivial matters.

Cornudet settled down beside the tall kitchen fireplace, before a blazing fire. He had a small table and a jug of beer placed beside him, and he smoked his pipe—a pipe which enjoyed among democrats a consideration almost equal to his own, as though it had served its country in serving Cornudet. It was a fine meerschaum, admirably colored to a black the shade of its owner's teeth, but sweet-smelling, gracefully curved, at home in its master's hand, and completing his physiognomy. And Cornudet sat motionless, his eyes fixed now on the dancing flames, now on the froth which crowned his beer; and after each draught he passed his long, thin fingers with an air of satisfaction through his long, greasy hair, as he sucked the foam from his mustache.

Loiseau, under pretence of stretching his legs, went out to see if he could sell wine to the country dealers. The count and the manufacturer began to talk politics. They forecast the future of France. One believed in the Orleans dynasty, the other in an unknown savior—a hero who should rise up in the last extremity: a Du Guesclin, perhaps a Joan of Arc? or another Napoléon the First? Ah! if only the Prince Imperial were not so young! Cornudet, listening to them, smiled like a man who holds the keys of destiny in his hands. His pipe perfumed the whole kitchen.

As the clock struck ten, Monsieur Follenvie appeared. He was immediately surrounded and questioned, but could only repeat, three or four times in succession, and without variation, the words:

"The officer said to me, just like this: 'Monsieur Follenvie, you will forbid them to harness up the coach for those travellers to-morrow. They are not to start without an order from me. You hear? That is sufficient.'"

Then they asked to see the officer. The count sent him his card, on which Monsieur Carre-Lamadon also inscribed his name and titles. The Prussian sent word that the two men would be admitted to see him after his luncheon—that is to say, about one o'clock.

The ladies reappeared, and they all ate a little, in spite of their anxiety. Boule de Suif appeared ill and very much worried.

They were finishing their coffee when the orderly came to fetch the gentlemen.

Loiseau joined the other two; but when they tried to get Cornudet to accompany them, by way of adding greater solemnity to the occasion, he declared proudly that he would never have anything to do with the Germans, and, resuming his seat in the chimney corner, he called for another jug of beer.

The three men went upstairs, and were ushered into the best room in the inn, where the officer received them lolling at his ease in an armchair, his feet on the mantelpiece, smoking a long porcelain pipe, and enveloped in a gorgeous dressing-gown, doubtless stolen from the deserted dwelling of some citizen destitute of taste in dress. He neither rose, greeted them, nor even glanced in their direction. He afforded a fine example of that insolence of bearing which seems natural to the victorious soldier.

After the lapse of a few moments he said in his halting French:

"What do you want?"

"We wish to start on our journey," said the count.

"No."

"May I ask the reason of your refusal?"

"Because I don't choose."

"I would respectfully call your attention, monsieur, to the fact that your general in command gave us a permit to proceed to Dieppe; and I do not think we have done anything to deserve this harshness at your hands."

"I don't choose — that's all. You may go."

They bowed, and retired.

The afternoon was wretched. They could not understand the caprice of this German, and the strangest ideas came into their heads. They all congregated in the kitchen, and talked the subject to death, imagining all kinds of unlikely things. Perhaps they were to be kept as hostages —but for what reason? or to be extradited as prisoners of war? or possibly they were to be held for ransom? They were panic-stricken at this last supposition. The richest among them were the most alarmed, seeing themselves forced to empty bags of gold into the insolent soldier's hands in order to buy back their lives. They racked their brains for plausible lies whereby they might conceal the fact that they were rich, and pass themselves off as poor — very poor. Loiseau took off his watch chain, and put it in his pocket. The approach of night increased their apprehension. The lamp was lighted, and as it wanted yet two hours to dinner Madame Loiseau proposed a game of trente et un. It would distract their thoughts. The rest agreed, and Cornudet himself joined the party, first putting out his pipe for politeness' sake.

The count shuffled the cards—dealt—and Boule de Suif had thirty-one to start with; soon the interest of the game assuaged the anxiety of the players. But Cornudet noticed that Loiseau and his wife were in league to cheat.

They were about to sit down to dinner when Monsieur Follenvie appeared, and in his grating voice announced:

"The Prussian officer sends to ask Mademoiselle Elisabeth Rousset if she has changed her mind yet."

Boule de Suif stood still, pale as death. Then, suddenly turning crimson with anger, she gasped out:

"Kindly tell that scoundrel, that cur, that carrion of a Prussian, that I will never consent—you understand?—never, never, never!"

The fat innkeeper left the room. Then Boule de Suif was surrounded, questioned, entreated on all sides to reveal the mystery of her visit to the officer. She refused at first; but her wrath soon got the better of her.

"What does he want? He wants to make me his mistress!" she cried.

No one was shocked at the word, so great was the general indignation. Cornudet broke his jug as he banged it down on the table. A loud outcry arose against this base soldier. All were furious. They drew together in common resistance against the foe, as if some part of the sacrifice exacted of Boule de Suif had been demanded of each. The count declared, with supreme disgust, that those people behaved like ancient barbarians. The women, above all, manifested a lively and tender sympathy for Boule de Suif. The nuns, who appeared only at meals, cast down their eyes, and said nothing.

They dined, however, as soon as the first indignant outburst had subsided; but they spoke little and thought much.

The ladies went to bed early; and the men, having lighted their pipes, proposed a game of ecarte, in which Monsieur Follenvie was invited to join, the travellers hoping to question him skillfully as to the best means of vanquishing the officer's obduracy. But he thought of nothing but his cards, would listen to nothing, reply to nothing, and repeated, time after time: "Attend to the game, gentlemen! attend to the game!" So absorbed was his attention that he even forgot to expectorate. The consequence was that his chest gave forth rumbling sounds like those of an organ. His wheezing lungs struck every note of the asthmatic scale, from deep, hollow tones to a shrill, hoarse piping resembling that of a young cock trying to crow.

He refused to go to bed when his wife, overcome with sleep, came to fetch him. So she went off alone, for she was an early bird, always up with the sun; while he was addicted to late hours, ever ready to spend the night with friends. He merely said: "Put my egg-nogg by the fire," and went on with the game. When the other men saw that nothing was to be got out of him they declared it was time to retire, and each sought his bed.

They rose fairly early the next morning, with a vague hope of being allowed to start, a greater desire than ever to do so, and a terror at having to spend another day in this wretched little inn.

Alas! the horses remained in the stable, the driver was invisible. They spent their time, for want of something better to do, in wandering round the coach.

Luncheon was a gloomy affair; and there was a general coolness toward Boule de Suif, for night, which brings counsel, had somewhat modified the judgment of her companions. In the cold light of the morning they almost bore a grudge against the girl for not having secretly sought out the Prussian, that the rest of the party might receive a joyful surprise when they awoke. What more simple?

Besides, who would have been the wiser? She might have saved appearances by telling the officer that she had taken pity on their distress. Such a step would be of so little consequence to her.

But no one as yet confessed to such thoughts.

In the afternoon, seeing that they were all bored to death, the count proposed a walk in the neighborhood of the village. Each one wrapped himself up well, and the little party set out, leaving behind only Cornudet, who preferred to sit over the fire, and the two nuns, who were in the habit of spending their day in the church or at the presbytery.

The cold, which grew more intense each day, almost froze the noses and ears of the pedestrians, their feet began to pain them so that each step was a penance, and when they reached the open country it looked so mournful and depressing in its limitless mantle of white that they all hastily retraced their steps, with bodies benumbed and hearts heavy.

The four women walked in front, and the three men followed a little in their rear.

Loiseau, who saw perfectly well how matters stood, asked suddenly "if that trollop were going to keep them waiting much longer in this Godforsaken spot." The count, always courteous, replied that they could not exact so painful a sacrifice from any woman, and that the first move must come from herself. Monsieur Carre-Lamadon remarked that if the French, as they talked of doing, made a counter attack by way of Dieppe, their encounter with the enemy must inevitably take place at Totes. This reflection made the other two anxious.

"Supposing we escape on foot?" said Loiseau.

The count shrugged his shoulders.

"How can you think of such a thing, in this snow? And with our wives? Besides, we should be pursued at once, overtaken in ten minutes, and brought back as prisoners at the mercy of the soldiery."

This was true enough; they were silent.

The ladies talked of dress, but a certain constraint seemed to prevail among them.

Suddenly, at the end of the street, the officer appeared. His tall, wasp-like, uniformed figure was outlined against the snow which bounded the horizon, and he walked, knees apart, with that motion peculiar to soldiers, who are always anxious not to soil their carefully polished boots.

He bowed as he passed the ladies, then glanced scornfully at the men, who had sufficient dignity not to raise their hats, though Loiseau made a movement to do so.

Boule de Suif flushed crimson to the ears, and the three married women felt unutterably humiliated at being met thus by the soldier in company with the girl whom he had treated with such scant ceremony.

Then they began to talk about him, his figure, and his face. Madame Carre-Lamadon, who had known many officers and judged them as a connoisseur, thought him not at all bad-looking; she even regretted that he was not a Frenchman, because in that case he would have made a very handsome hussar, with whom all the women would assuredly have fallen in love.

When they were once more within doors they did not know what to do with themselves. Sharp words even were exchanged apropos of the merest trifles. The silent dinner was quickly over, and each one went to bed early in the hope of sleeping, and thus killing time.

They came down next morning with tired faces and irritable tempers; the women scarcely spoke to Boule de Suif.

A church bell summoned the faithful to a baptism. Boule de Suif had a child being brought up by peasants at Yvetot. She did not see him once a year, and never thought of him; but the idea of the child who was about to be baptized induced a sudden wave of tenderness for her own, and she insisted on being present at the ceremony.

As soon as she had gone out, the rest of the company looked at one another and then drew their chairs together; for they realized that they must decide on some course of action. Loiseau had an inspiration: he proposed that they should ask the officer to detain Boule de Suif only, and to let the rest depart on their way.

Monsieur Follenvie was intrusted with this commission, but he returned to them almost immediately. The German, who knew human nature, had shown him the door. He intended to keep all the travellers until his condition had been complied with.

Whereupon Madame Loiseau's vulgar temperament broke bounds.

"We're not going to die of old age here!" she cried. "Since it's that vixen's trade to behave so with men I don't see that she has any right to refuse one more than another. I may as well tell you she took any lovers she could get at Rouen—even coachmen! Yes, indeed, madame—the coachman at the prefecture! I know it for a fact, for he buys his wine of us. And now that it is a question of getting us out of a difficulty she puts on virtuous airs, the drab! For my part, I think this officer has behaved very well. Why, there were three others of us, any one of whom he would undoubtedly have preferred. But no, he contents himself with the girl who is common property. He respects married women. Just think. He is master here. He had only to say: 'I wish it!' and he might have taken us by force, with the help of his soldiers."

The two other women shuddered; the eyes of pretty Madame Carre-Lamadon glistened, and she grew pale, as if the officer were indeed in the act of laying violent hands on her.

The men, who had been discussing the subject among themselves, drew near. Loiseau, in a state of furious resentment, was for delivering up "that miserable woman," bound hand and foot, into the enemy's power. But the count, descended from three generations of ambassadors, and endowed, moreover, with the lineaments of a diplomat, was in favor of more tactful measures.

"We must persuade her," he said.

Then they laid their plans.

The women drew together; they lowered their voices, and the discussion became general, each giving his or her opinion. But the conversation was not in the least coarse. The ladies, in particular, were adepts at delicate phrases and charming subtleties of expression to describe the most improper things. A stranger would have understood none of their allusions, so guarded was the language they employed. But, seeing that the thin veneer of modesty with which every woman of the world is furnished goes but a very little way below the surface, they began rather to enjoy this unedifying episode, and at bottom were hugely delighted —feeling themselves in their element, furthering the schemes of lawless love with the gusto of a gourmand cook who prepares supper for another.

Their gaiety returned of itself, so amusing at last did

the whole business seem to them. The count uttered several rather risky witticisms, but so tactfully were they said that his audience could not help smiling. Loiseau in turn made some considerably broader jokes, but no one took offence; and the thought expressed with such brutal directness by his wife was uppermost in the minds of all: "Since it's the girl's trade, why should she refuse this man more than another?" Dainty Madame Carre-Lamadon seemed to think even that in Boule de Suif's place she would be less inclined to refuse him than another.

The blockade was as carefully arranged as if they were investing a fortress. Each agreed on the role which he or she was to play, the arguments to be used, the maneuvers to be executed. They decided on the plan of campaign, the stratagems they were to employ, and the surprise attacks which were to reduce this human citadel and force it to receive the enemy within its walls.

But Cornudet remained apart from the rest, taking no share in the plot.

So absorbed was the attention of all that Boule de Suif's entrance was almost unnoticed. But the count whispered a gentle "Hush!" which made the others look up. She was there. They suddenly stopped talking, and a vague embarrassment prevented them for a few moments from addressing her. But the countess, more practiced than the others in the wiles of the room, asked her:

"Was the baptism interesting?"

The girl, still under the stress of emotion, told what she had seen and heard, described the faces, the attitudes of those present, and even the appearance of the church. She concluded with the words:

"It does one good to pray sometimes."

Until lunch time the ladies contented themselves with being pleasant to her, so as to increase her confidence and make her amenable to their advice.

As soon as they took their seats at table the attack began. First they opened a vague conversation on the subject of self-sacrifice. Ancient examples were quoted: Judith and Holofernes; then, irrationally enough, Lucrece and Sextus; Cleopatra and the hostile generals whom she reduced to abject slavery by a surrender of her charms. Next was recounted an extraordinary story, born of the imagination of these ignorant millionaires, which told how the matrons of Rome seduced Hannibal, his lieutenants, and all his mercenaries at Capua. They held up to admiration all those women who from time to time have arrested the victorious progress of conquerors, made of their bodies a field of battle, a means of ruling, a weapon; who have vanquished by their heroic caresses hideous or detested beings, and sacrificed their chastity to vengeance and devotion.

All was said with due restraint and regard for propriety, the effect heightened now and then by an outburst of forced enthusiasm calculated to excite emulation.

A listener would have thought at last that the one role of woman on earth was a perpetual sacrifice of her person, a continual abandonment of herself to the caprices of a hostile soldiery.

The two nuns seemed to hear nothing, and to be lost in thought. Boule de Suif also was silent.

During the whole afternoon she was left to her reflections. But instead of calling her "madame" as they had done hitherto, her companions addressed her simply as "mademoiselle," without exactly knowing why, but as if desirous of making her descend a step in the esteem she had won, and forcing her to realize her degraded position.

Just as soup was served, Monsieur Follenvie reappeared, repeating his phrase of the evening before:

"The Prussian officer sends to ask if Mademoiselle Elisabeth Rousset has changed her mind."

Boule de Suif answered briefly:

"No, monsieur."

But at dinner the coalition weakened. Loiseau made three unfortunate remarks. Each was cudgeling his brains for further examples of self-sacrifice, and could find none, when the countess, possibly without ulterior motive, and moved simply by a vague desire to do homage to religion, began to question the elder of the two nuns on the most striking facts in the lives of the saints. Now, it fell out that many of these had committed acts which would be crimes in our eyes, but the Church readily pardons such deeds when they are accomplished for the glory of God or the good of mankind. This was a powerful argument, and the countess made the most of it. Then, whether by reason of a tacit understanding, a thinly veiled act of complaisance such as those who wear the ecclesiastical habit excel in, or whether merely as the result of sheer stupidity—a stupidity admirably adapted to further their designs—the old nun rendered formidable aid to the conspirator. They had thought her timid; she proved herself bold, talkative, bigoted. She was not troubled by the ins and outs of casuistry; her doctrines were as iron bars; her faith knew no doubt; her conscience no scruples. She looked on Abraham's sacrifice as natural enough, for she herself would not have hesitated to kill both father and mother if she had received a divine order to that effect; and nothing, in her opinion, could displease our Lord, provided the motive were praiseworthy. The countess, putting to good use the consecrated authority of her unexpected ally, led

her on to make a lengthy and edifying paraphrase of
that axiom enunciated by a certain school of moralists:
"The end justifies the means."

"Then, sister," she asked, "you think God accepts all
methods, and pardons the act when the motive is pure?"

"Undoubtedly, madame. An action reprehensible
in itself often derives merit from the thought which
inspires it."

And in this wise they talked on, fathoming the wishes
of God, predicting His judgments, describing Him as
interested in matters which assuredly concern Him
but little.

All was said with the utmost care and discretion, but
every word uttered by the holy woman in her nun's garb
weakened the indignant resistance of the courtesan.
Then the conversation drifted somewhat, and the
nun began to talk of the convents of her order, of her
Superior, of herself, and of her fragile little neighbor,
Sister St. Nicephore. They had been sent for from
Havre to nurse the hundreds of soldiers who were in
hospitals, stricken with smallpox. She described these
wretched invalids and their malady. And, while they
themselves were detained on their way by the caprices
of the Prussian officer, scores of Frenchmen might be
dying, whom they would otherwise have saved! For
the nursing of soldiers was the old nun's specialty; she

had been in the Crimea, in Italy, in Austria; and as she told the story of her campaigns she revealed herself as one of those holy sisters of the fife and drum who seem designed by nature to follow camps, to snatch the wounded from amid the strife of battle, and to quell with a word, more effectually than any general, the rough and insubordinate troopers—a masterful woman, her seamed and pitted face itself an image of the devastations of war.

No one spoke when she had finished for fear of spoiling the excellent effect of her words.

As soon as the meal was over the travellers retired to their rooms, whence they emerged the following day at a late hour of the morning.

Luncheon passed off quietly. The seed sown the preceding evening was being given time to germinate and bring forth fruit.

In the afternoon the countess proposed a walk; then the count, as had been arranged beforehand, took Boule de Suif's arm, and walked with her at some distance behind the rest.

He began talking to her in that familiar, paternal, slightly contemptuous tone which men of his class adopt in speaking to women like her, calling her "my dear child," and talking down to her from the height of his exalted social position and stainless reputation. He came straight to the point.

"So you prefer to leave us here, exposed like yourself to all the violence which would follow on a repulse of the Prussian troops, rather than consent to surrender yourself, as you have done so many times in your life?"

The girl did not reply.

He tried kindness, argument, sentiment. He still bore himself as count, even while adopting, when desirable, an attitude of gallantry, and making pretty—nay, even tender—speeches. He exalted the service she would render them, spoke of their gratitude; then, suddenly, using the familiar "thou":

"And you know, my dear, he could boast then of having made a conquest of a pretty girl such as he won't often find in his own country."

Boule de Suif did not answer, and joined the rest of the party.

As soon as they returned she went to her room, and was seen no more. The general anxiety was at its height. What would she do? If she still resisted, how awkward for them all!

The dinner hour struck; they waited for her in vain. At last Monsieur Follenvie entered, announcing that Mademoiselle Rousset was not well, and that they might sit down to table. They all pricked up their ears. The count drew near the innkeeper, and whispered:

"Is it all right?"

"Yes."

Out of regard for propriety he said nothing to his companions, but merely nodded slightly toward them. A great sigh of relief went up from all breasts; every face was lighted up with joy.

"By Gad!" shouted Loiseau, "I'll stand champagne all round if there's any to be found in this place." And great was Madame Loiseau's dismay when the proprietor came back with four bottles in his hands. They had all suddenly become talkative and merry; a lively joy filled all hearts. The count seemed to perceive for the first time that Madame Carre-Lamadon was charming; the manufacturer paid compliments to the countess. The conversation was animated, sprightly, witty, and, although many of the jokes were in the worst possible taste, all the company were amused by them, and none offended—indignation being dependent, like other emotions, on surroundings. And the mental atmosphere had gradually become filled with gross imaginings and unclean thoughts.

At dessert even the women indulged in discreetly worded allusions. Their glances were full of meaning; they had drunk much. The count, who even in his moments of relaxation preserved a dignified demeanor, hit on a much-appreciated comparison of the condition of things with the termination of a winter spent in the icy solitude of the North Pole and the joy of shipwrecked mariners who at last perceive a southward track opening out before their eyes.

Loiseau, fairly in his element, rose to his feet, holding aloft a glass of champagne.

"I drink to our deliverance!" he shouted.

All stood up, and greeted the toast with acclamation. Even the two good sisters yielded to the solicitations of the ladies, and consented to moisten their lips with the foaming wine, which they had never before tasted. They declared it was like effervescent lemonade, but with a pleasanter flavor.

"It is a pity," said Loiseau, "that we have no piano; we might have had a quadrille."

Cornudet had not spoken a word or made a movement; he seemed plunged in serious thought, and now and then tugged furiously at his great beard, as if trying to add still further to its length. At last, toward midnight, when they were about to separate, Loiseau, whose gait was far from steady, suddenly slapped him on the back, saying thickly:

"You're not jolly to-night; why are you so silent, old man?"

Cornudet threw back his head, cast one swift and scornful glance over the assemblage, and answered:

"I tell you all, you have done an infamous thing!"

He rose, reached the door, and repeating: "Infamous!" disappeared.

A chill fell on all. Loiseau himself looked foolish and disconcerted for a moment, but soon recovered his aplomb, and, writhing with laughter, exclaimed:

"Really, you are all too green for anything!"

Pressed for an explanation, he related the "mysteries of the corridor," whereat his listeners were hugely amused. The ladies could hardly contain their delight. The count and Monsieur Carre-Lamadon laughed till they cried. They could scarcely believe their ears.

"What! you are sure? He wanted — —"

"I tell you I saw it with my own eyes."

"And she refused?"

"Because the Prussian was in the next room!"

"Surely you are mistaken?"

"I swear I'm telling you the truth."

The count was choking with laughter. The manufacturer held his sides. Loiseau continued:

"So you may well imagine he doesn't think this evening's business at all amusing."

And all three began to laugh again, choking, coughing, almost ill with merriment.

Then they separated. But Madame Loiseau, who was nothing if not spiteful, remarked to her husband as they were on the way to bed that "that stuck-up little minx of a Carre-Lamadon had laughed on the wrong side of her mouth all the evening."

"You know," she said, "when women run after uniforms it's all the same to them whether the men who wear them are French or Prussian. It's perfectly sickening!"

The next morning the snow showed dazzling white tinder a clear winter sun. The coach, ready at last, waited before the door; while a flock of white pigeons, with pink eyes spotted in the centres with black, puffed out their white feathers and walked sedately between the legs of the six horses, picking at the steaming manure.

The driver, wrapped in his sheepskin coat, was smoking a pipe on the box, and all the passengers, radiant with delight at their approaching departure, were putting up provisions for the remainder of the journey.

They were waiting only for Boule de Suif. At last she appeared.

She seemed rather shamefaced and embarrassed, and advanced with timid step toward her companions, who with one accord turned aside as if they had not seen her. The count, with much dignity, took his wife by the arm, and removed her from the unclean contact.

The girl stood still, stupefied with astonishment; then, plucking up courage, accosted the manufacturer's wife with a humble "Good-morning, madame," to which the other replied merely with a slight and insolent nod, accompanied by a look of outraged virtue. Every one suddenly appeared extremely busy, and kept as far from Boule de Suif as if tier skirts had been infected with some deadly disease. Then they hurried to the coach, followed by the despised courtesan, who, arriving last of all, silently took the place she had occupied during the first part of the journey.

The rest seemed neither to see nor to know her—all save Madame Loiseau, who, glancing contemptuously in her direction, remarked, half aloud, to her husband:

"What a mercy I am not sitting beside that creature!"

The lumbering vehicle started on its way, and the journey began afresh.

At first no one spoke. Boule de Suif dared not even raise her eyes. She felt at once indignant with her neighbors, and humiliated at having yielded to the Prussian into whose arms they had so hypocritically cast her.

But the countess, turning toward Madame Carre-Lamadon, soon broke the painful silence:

"I think you know Madame d'Etrelles?"

"Yes; she is a friend of mine."

"Such a charming woman!"

"Delightful! Exceptionally talented, and an artist to the finger tips. She sings marvellously and draws to perfection."

The manufacturer was chatting with the count, and amid the clatter of the window-panes a word of their conversation was now and then distinguishable: "Shares—maturity—premium—time-limit."

Loiseau, who had abstracted from the inn the timeworn pack of cards, thick with the grease of five years' contact with half-wiped-off tables, started a game of bezique with his wife.

The good sisters, taking up simultaneously the long rosaries hanging from their waists, made the sign of the cross, and began to mutter in unison interminable prayers, their lips moving ever more and more swiftly, as if they sought which should outdistance the other in the race of orisons; from time to time they kissed a medal, and crossed themselves anew, then resumed their rapid and unintelligible murmur.

Cornudet sat still, lost in thought.

Ah the end of three hours Loiseau gathered up the cards, and remarked that he was hungry.

His wife thereupon produced a parcel tied with string, from which she extracted a piece of cold veal. This she cut into neat, thin slices, and both began to eat.

"We may as well do the same," said the countess. The rest agreed, and she unpacked the provisions which had been prepared for herself, the count, and the Carre-Lamadons. In one of those oval dishes, the lids of which are decorated with an earthenware hare, by way of showing that a game pie lies within, was a succulent delicacy consisting of the brown flesh of the game larded with streaks of bacon and flavored with other meats chopped fine. A solid wedge of Gruyere cheese, which had been wrapped in a newspaper, bore the imprint: "Items of News," on its rich, oily surface.

The two good sisters brought to light a hunk of sausage smelling strongly of garlic; and Cornudet, plunging both hands at once into the capacious pockets of his loose overcoat, produced from one four hard-boiled eggs and from the other a crust of bread. He removed the shells, threw them into the straw beneath his feet, and began to devour the eggs, letting morsels of the bright yellow yolk fall in his mighty beard, where they looked like stars.

Boule de Suif, in the haste and confusion of her

departure, had not thought of anything, and, stifling with rage, she watched all these people placidly eating. At first, ill-suppressed wrath shook her whole person, and she opened her lips to shriek the truth at them, to overwhelm them with a volley of insults; but she could not utter a word, so choked was she with indignation.

No one looked at her, no one thought of her. She felt herself swallowed up in the scorn of these virtuous creatures, who had first sacrificed, then rejected her as a thing useless and unclean. Then she remembered her big basket full of the good things they had so greedily devoured: the two chickens coated in jelly, the pies, the pears, the four bottles of claret; and her fury broke forth like a cord that is overstrained, and she was on the verge of tears. She made terrible efforts at self-control, drew herself up, swallowed the sobs which choked her; but the tears rose nevertheless, shone at the brink of her eyelids, and soon two heavy drops coursed slowly down her cheeks. Others followed more quickly, like water filtering from a rock, and fell, one after another, on her rounded bosom. She sat upright, with a fixed expression, her face pale and rigid, hoping desperately that no one saw her give way.

But the countess noticed that she was weeping, and with a sign drew her husband's attention to the fact. He shrugged his shoulders, as if to say: "Well, what of it? It's not my fault." Madame Loiseau chuckled triumphantly, and murmured:

"She's weeping for shame."

The two nuns had betaken themselves once more to their prayers, first wrapping the remainder of their sausage in paper:

Then Cornudet, who was digesting his eggs, stretched his long legs under the opposite seat, threw himself back, folded his arms, smiled like a man who had just thought of a good joke, and began to whistle the Marseillaise.

The faces of his neighbors clouded; the popular air evidently did not find favor with them; they grew nervous and irritable, and seemed ready to howl as a dog does at the sound of a barrel-organ. Cornudet saw the discomfort he was creating, and whistled the louder; sometimes he even hummed the words:

> *Amour sacre de la patrie,*
> *Conduis, soutiens, nos bras vengeurs,*
> *Liberte, liberte cherie,*
> *Combats avec tes defenseurs!*

The coach progressed more swiftly, the snow being harder now; and all the way to Dieppe, during the long, dreary hours of the journey, first in the gathering dusk, then in the thick darkness, raising his voice above the rumbling of the vehicle, Cornudet continued with fierce obstinacy his vengeful and monotonous whistling, forcing his weary and exasperated-hearers to follow the song from end to end, to recall every word of every line, as each was repeated over and over again with untiring persistency.

And Boule de Suif still wept, and sometimes a sob she could not restrain was heard in the darkness between two verses of the song.

The end

Printing: CreateSpace
Charleston SC, in may 2017.

Printed in USA.

Cover :

Pierre-Auguste Renoir,
« Portrait of Jeanne Samary » (1877).
Pushkin State Museum of Fine Arts, Moscow (Russia).

Made in the USA
Middletown, DE
31 October 2018